THE BOSS BIAS

An Age Gap, Curvy Girl Romance

Hallie Bennett

The Arrowed Heart

BOOKS BY THIS AUTHOR

Batter Up: An Instalove, Curvy Girl Romance

Wood Lessons: An Instalove,
Curvy Girl Romance

Tees & Jeans Series

The Brother Bias: *A Brother's Best*
Friend, Curvy Girl Romance

The Boss Bias: *An Age Gap,*
Curvy Girl Romance

The Bad Boy Bias: *An Opposites*
Attract, Curvy Girl Romance

CONTENTS

PROLOGUE

SAOIRSE

Pink and red streamers line Main Street for the Valentine's Day Festival as Abigail, Ella, and I amble along the crowded sidewalk. We're here to enjoy one of the few large events Smithfield hosts along with one other very specific task — to try our luck at finding love.

"There it is. I found it!" Ella points excitedly at a booth decked out in holiday paraphernalia: cupids, hearts, teddy bears — the works. Destination sighted, we weave through groups of people to head that way.

The Smithfield Matchmaking Booth.

Each year we'd talk about signing up but could never muster the guts to follow through with the plan. A trio of curvy introverts, we met in college and formed a club where we promised to remain true to ourselves and never change for attention. Calling ourselves the Tees and Jeans Club, the spirit of the club has remained, though we've branched out from our casual uniform.

"So we're really doing this?" Abigail asks, hugging her cardigan closer. The quietest of us, her nerves are obvious.

"Yes, we are; it's been decided." I twine my arm through hers while holding a cup of apple cider tight in my other hand. "We'll be thirty soon, and it's time we take charge of our destinies." All of us have trouble talking with guys — not that our small town teems with single, attractive men. But if it did, we'd still be hiding on the sidelines. At least with the matchmaking booth, we might have a chance. It's a blind match with all conversations occurring via letter; maybe the anonymity will help us shed our inhibitions.

To be honest, I'm already reaching that point after years of singlehood. Right after graduation, I'd ridden the confidence boost of surviving college and landing a job so quickly into a one-night stand with a fellow graduate to rid myself of my virginity. But no relationship followed from him or anyone else and call it what you will, but the older I get the less I care about how guys perceive me.

I want a man. Plain and simple. Someone to love, to build a life with, and to yeah, *fuck*.

My current way of living? Not working for me, so sign me up for matchmaking.

Cold February air serrates my

lungs as I take another deep breath for courage and wonder who my match could be. Like I said, troves of available men don't cross my path very often, so where will the eligible bachelors for matchmaking come from?

As if to challenge that thought, a handsome man brushes by us, and my eyes follow briefly before returning to our course. *That's one.*

"Hello, ladies. Are the three of you interested in participating this year?" An older woman in a blush-colored sweater stands to greet us, her pink-tinged hair suiting the booth's theme perfectly.

We let out a resounding "Yes" at varying degrees of excitement. Huddling nearer to the table filled with pictures of happy couples and packets of paperwork, I send up a quick prayer that this works.

"How lovely! We've got a great selection of singles, so I'm sure we'll find perfect matches for everyone." Collecting three clipboards with a stack of forms, she hands one to each of us. "Now, fill these out, and when you're done, I'll go over what happens next."

I take a seat next to Ella on a bench and start writing in answers to the extensive questionnaire — beginning with a pseudonym instead of using my real name for the correspondence. Tapping the pen against my cheek, names filter through my mind until I decide to go the simple route and use a play on my name.

The rest of the questions are more in-depth than I would expect from a small-town festival attraction, but I suppose it's good that they're being thorough. Maybe that means this will actually result in a relationship.

Give me your best shot , Cupid.

Once we finish and turn in the sheets, the woman explains the process. "We'll try our best to match everyone as well as we can, though sometimes we have odd numbers or someone needs a special fit that we can't meet. The letters are all anonymous."

She points to the scribbled writing on our forms before motioning to an address on a brochure. "You'll use the names you chose on the form and mail the letters to the matchmaking P.O. box. We'll make sure everyone's letters get to the right person. The point of this process is to get to know someone completely blind until you reach a point where you're willing to meet in person, then we step out as mediators and give you the information you need to continue. Make sense?"

We nod and take the folder of information she hands over at the end of her spiel. "What's your success rate?" I ask curiously, trying to gauge how much I should temper my hopes.

"We usually have a couple hundred people enter and half of those go on to meet in person. Once that happens, we've seen thirty percent of couples make it to engagements and marriage. Keep in mind, this booth has only been up and running for three years, but I'm proud of the connections we've made so far."

Thirty percent.

Not terrible, especially if I compare it to something like the Bachelor or Bachelorette; that show has a terrible success rate yet keeps chugging along. Maybe I'll be one of the lucky ones.

After all, I've got Irish in my blood.

CHAPTER ONE

SAOIRSE

EIGHT MONTHS LATER

Liberty,

My new position comes with its challenges, but it's nothing I can't handle. I'm a bit of a thrill seeker, I suppose, because overhauling moldering systems, pulling them back from the brink, gives me a rush like no other. Well, except for you, of course.

Your letters are the highlight of my days, and the pictures you send... My cock thanks you, though my hand gets tired.

I want to see my sexy pin-up girl.

Tell me we can finally meet. Your name means "freedom", so please release me from this torture and say "Yes."

Your devoted (and very horny) servant,

Law

I finish reading my anonymous match's letter, carefully refolding it and adding the sheet to the rest of his correspondence. Sometimes sweet, sometimes lusty — he always makes me blush. Who knew I'd be so fortunate after signing up for the matchmaking service?

Poor Abigail and Ella's matches had fizzled out after a couple of letters, but mine remains strong. And it's become much more than writing down thoughts and feelings. I've escalated to including naughty polaroids for his pleasure; he wasn't lying by calling me his 'sexy pin-up girl'. The anonymity of our connection allows me to explore a side I rarely show others — the part that wants to be seen and desired.

Though we're meant to eventually move budding relationships into the open, there's a wall in my mind preventing me from taking that next step. I like living in this fantasy. Of never having to worry what Law will truly think of me because we keep it strictly confined to letters and photos.

With that in mind, I'd mustered up my courage and started snapping pictures of myself in silk and lace lingerie, making sure to never show my face but give him a taste of what he could have — if I ever worked up the courage to meet in person. Not to mention, it intensified my own foreplay preparing for the photoshoots.

Damn, did it make me feel powerful.

I don't want to lose that feeling by entering into reality and having him see me in all my glory without prepared angles grabbing the best shots. It would hurt too much — no matter how confident I've grown with his encouragement and praise. I don't want to disappoint him or revert back to the woman too nervous to speak with a man, let alone share suggestive photos. And I definitely don't want this strong connection between us to wither because ordinary dating isn't as romantic as these letters.

Adjusting the camera angle for my next shot, I tease my nipples into hard points that poke at the thin silk of my nightgown before arching my back, causing the fabric to pull tighter against my breasts. The timer clicks, and a photo spits out with a familiar hum. Rolling to my stomach, I snatch the picture and shake it before an image appears.

Perfect.

My aroused body on display for Law will be sure to satisfy him for the time being; I'm just not sure how long it will last. His eagerness to meet is understandable; it's been months of writing to each other. And I do wonder what he looks like — who he is.

Every time I'm at the grocery store and see a man alone, questions of "Is he the one?" pop up. Then, like a hypocrite, I fear not being attracted to him despite our emotional connection.

Another reason to stay safe in the bubble of anonymity.

Sliding the photo in an envelope, I write a letter in response to his — making excuses to hold him at bay. One of these days, I'll agree to meet, but it won't be anytime soon.

And definitely not this week with all the preparations I need to do for work. Dropping the letter in the basket holding my keys by the door, my mind switches gears, and I go over the list of things to get done tomorrow.

It's Homecoming Week at Smithfield College. As the manager of the campus cafe, which serves as a host for all guests, I need to keep the cafe completely staffed —   maneuvering around students' special schedules this week — along with double-checking we have enough inventory to accommodate such an influx of visitors.

Plus, the college has a new Vice President of Finances, and he's chosen this week to inspect my work and budget. To be fair, I think he's working alphabetically down a list of names, but it sucks that my name falls on one of the busiest weeks of the year for me.

Curling into the plush arm of my couch, my hand flies across the page of my work notebook, listing what needs to be checked and adding reminders for what to prepare for Mr. Moore's visit tomorrow. Despite the small size of campus, I've only seen glimpses of him in passing and haven't heard much gossip which is strange. An older man with salt and pepper hair, he's still attractive — the women in Admissions would usually be pretty chatty about someone like him.

Maybe he's married.

I shake my head in amusement because that wouldn't stop them from admiring him and decided that whatever he is — married or single — I hope he's reasonable and won't start telling me how to do a job I've done well for the past six years.

Because I don't take kindly to being told what to do — even if he is my boss now.

CHAPTER TWO

THOMAS

I wake with a groan as my hand continues squeezing my morning wood, waking from another dream of Liberty — my mystery match and the woman starring in all of my fantasies. *If only I had a face to put with her gorgeous body...*

Eight months and nothing more than barely-covered curves or the back of her head showcasing long, fiery curls.

She keeps putting me off, never agreeing to an official date — no matter how hard I push. And I'm not sure how to get past her hesitation.

When I'd signed up at the matchmaking booth last winter, my expectations had been low, but friends kept harassing me to get out there, so I gave in — never thinking it would actually work. The first letter I received from Liberty had been sweet and full of trepidation, and the next had been a little more relaxed, a little more trusting. Until she felt comfortable opening up to me about her past: the strong bond she shares with her college friends, the lonely road of singleness that led her to sign up for matchmaking. As we continued exchanging our fears and dreams for the future, it eventually morphed into what we have now.

I'll never forget that first photo she sent me; I felt like a teenager as many times as I jerked off to the view of her lush breasts spilling out of a scarlet red teddy in honor of the Fourth of July. A man my age should have more control, but how could I resist?

An alarm beeps from the night-stand, and I try to set aside thoughts of Liberty in favor of the mountain of work I have ahead of me. Taking over from a predecessor who'd checked out of the job years prior to their retire-ment sucked. I love challenges which is what drew me to this new position, but fuck, some of these department heads refuse to adapt to better systems — insisting on clinging to old ways that aren't fiscally working anymore. Hopefully, my meetings today won't be so contentious.

The morning passes in a blur of showering, shaving, and breakfast be-fore I drive the short distance to a campus decked out in blue and gold for Homecoming Week. While I didn't attend Smithfield College, the school spirit is catching, and I'm looking forward to the soccer game versus our rival on Friday. It's strange not having a football game mark the end of the week, but we're too small to substantiate such a team — thus, soccer reigns supreme.

"Good morning, Kelsey." I greet my personal assistant upon walking into the shared space housing mine and the Vice President of Operations' offices.

"Morning, Mr. Moore." She smiles brightly and stands, revealing her short skirt. "Is there anything I can get you?"

"No, thank you." I dismiss the offer and continue walking. Since my arrival, Kelsey's made her interest known, though I've kept things professional. There's already a woman in my life, even if she's not physically present yet.

Fingers crossed that changes soon...

A couple of students cut by in the student center as I head downstairs to the campus cafe known as The Bean — my last stop for the day, thankfully. Everyone has been resistant to the slightest suggestion, and I'm ready to go home and reread Liberty's letters in an effort to relax.

But first: Saoirse Shane.

I don't know much about her other than the fact that she manages the cafe, and according to the numbers I've seen, she seems more competent than some of her colleagues. Honestly, this should just be a cursory walk-through, since the books look good.

The sharp aroma of coffee surrounds me as I step into the dim shop, ignoring the "Closed" sign hanging on the door. Hidden in the basement of the student center, small windows looking out on a gravel parking lot allow minimal light inside. But I can tell someone spent considerable effort trying to brighten the space with colorful paint and framed art on the concrete walls.

A woman perches on a step ladder, struggling to erase something from the top corner of the chalkboard menu. Her precarious position worries me, and I immediately circle the counter to provide back-up.

"Excuse me —"

"Sorry, we're closed during dinner, but you're welcome to come back around eight when we open again." Her voice is labored as she tries stretching for the out-of-reach spot again.

"I'm not a student. I'm Thomas Moore, VP of Finances." My hand hovers over her lower back, ready to catch her at the barest hint of a slip. "I really think you should let me help before you fall and hurt yourself."

"Fuck." The quiet whisper isn't meant for my ears, I'm sure, but a smile tugs on my mouth at the soft expletive. "I apologize for the unconventional introduction; I thought I had a few more minutes before you'd be here."

She scurries down the ladder, jumping off the last step with a hop, and turns to face me. "I'm...Saoirse." Her green eyes widen at our proximity as her name stutters out after an awkward pause. Lemon cuts through the coffee in the air, and I realize the tart sweetness is coming from her before giving her some space.

There's a familiarity about her, but I shake the odd notion. So she has red curls like my Liberty — doesn't mean a thing. Lots of women share the same trait.

"No problem. Let me erase that section for you, then we can take a look through your budget and be done. Shouldn't take more than fifteen minutes." I grab the rag she dropped on the counter, gently guiding her to the side as I climb the ladder to finish the task. "You've done a great job with The Bean, especially since you inherited a mess, from what I can tell."

"Thank you. Mrs. Landry did the best she could, but it was a relief when I was able to take over."

"You knew the previous manager?" I ask, two feet on the floor again and curious to hear how she landed her supervisory position when she looks so young. Freckles sprinkle across her nose and cheeks enforcing the youthful image.

"Oh, yeah." She nods and waves me back into the kitchen area where I follow her to a small desk with a laptop. "I used to work here as a barista when I attended Smithfield. When Mrs. Landry decided to leave, she asked if I wanted the job once I graduated. It kind of fell into my lap; I didn't even interview for it. But it's been a fun experience that's taught me a lot."

Taking a seat, she clicks around on the screen until a spreadsheet pops up. "Sorry, I'm kind of rambling. Here are the numbers for the semester so far." Saoirse slides to the right, so I can look over her shoulder to study the figures — something I've already checked in my office.

"Like I said, you're doing great. Better than a lot of the other departments, but let's keep that between us." I joke and move back a little.

She laughs and crosses her heart. "Your secret's safe. I'm just happy to hear the cafe's in the clear." Shrugging her denim jacket off, a navy tank reveals bare shoulders and a mark catches my eye — light brown and unmistakable. The blood drains from my face as my muscles tense.

And one word storms through the explosion of emotions firing in my body.

"Liberty?"

CHAPTER THREE

SAOIRSE

My heart stops at the sound of my pseudonym — only one person could know that name: Law.

My mystery match is Mr. Moore?

The same man who is my new boss?

"Law?" Disbelief laces my tone, and I half-hope he denies the moniker, however ridiculous the notion.

"So, it is you... Christ!" He runs a hand over his short hair, dark eyes travelling over my body. "I've seen… You sent… Fuck, how old are you?"

"Twenty-eight. You?"

Another curse bursts from him. "Too old, that's for damn sure."

"Hardly." The only outward signs of his age are the silver flecks in his hair and laugh lines around his eyes. Otherwise, Law — Thomas… Mr. Moore? — looked fit and fine in his button down shirt and dress pants. Like a switch has flipped, the shock of discovering my boss is my match morphs into a flood of desire. It's unsettling and makes my head spin. No longer is he just an attractive stranger.

This is *my* man — older, more experienced. And the daddy kink of it all kicks up the heat gathering between my thighs, obliterating rational thought. My eyes drink in his tall form, and I'm glad we're alone because all sorts of dirty ideas are swirling in my head. Stepping closer, I brazenly run a hand up his chest. "I don't mind an older man. In fact, it turns me on."

"Liberty... Saoirse. Age aside, I'm still technically your boss. This is inappropriate." But he doesn't push me away, his hand just covers mine, holding it to his heart.

"I think it adds spice. We'll have our own naughty little secret." I'm not sure what's come over me, the fear I harbored about meeting in person dissipated to be replaced by this confident seductress. Maybe all of those empowering boudoir shots boosted my self-esteem more than I thought.

That and all of the smutty books you read with Ella and Abigail.

"That risks our jobs. Which wouldn't be as much of a problem if you'd agreed to meet me months ago like I wanted."

"How do you figure?" My brows furrow at the blame placed on me. It's not my fault we work for the same college now; clearly, fate had something up her sleeve.

"If we'd met, I never would have taken this job placing me in a position of power over you." Images of him over me multiply like bunnies, and I lick my lips before focusing on his own firm mouth.

"You're the only one who has a problem with the situation. I don't mind your being in charge... at least for part of the time. Maybe I need to prove to you how little I care?"

Leaning forward, I press my mouth to his — awe at the bold move races through my blood. As first kisses go, I never expected ours to be initiated by me, but it suits the power dynamic I'm riding at the moment. I'm not usually a take-charge person, but I feel safe with Thomas despite his current resistance. We may not have met in person until now, but through our letters, I've learned who he is — someone I can trust and someone who wants me, no matter how hard he's trying to fight it. It seems crazy to make the jump so fast, but fear is the last thing on my mind at the moment.

Desire. Lust. Thomas. Those are the only things occupying my thoughts.

Months of pent-up desire flows between us as we finally give in to the other. Swiping my tongue over his lips, a hand squeezes my hip in reaction as a groan erupts from him, mouth opening to let me in. He tastes like coffee from his afternoon cup: rich and decadent. Perfect for a cafe manager who's become a sort of connoisseur of such things over the years. Wrapping my arms around his neck, I pull myself deeper into him, our tongues dueling as I rub my suddenly aching breasts against his chest.

I want to rub my whole body against his like a cat in heat, but common sense prevails that a kiss is as far as we can go for the time being.

"Easy, little girl." And the endearment almost makes me come right there.

Yes, Daddy.

The term forms easily like I was meant to call him that name. Thomas edges us apart, his thumb resting on my bottom lip, and I flick the tip of it with my tongue, eliciting a warning growl from him. "Behave. Anyone can discover us down here, then we'll both be fucked."

"My employees' next shift doesn't start for another few hours, so I can definitely get on board with us being fucked." I don't live too far from campus; it wouldn't be too difficult to get home for privacy — free to explore the muscles bunching beneath my hands.

An exasperated chuckle vibrates from him as he shakes his head. "I should've known you'd be trouble based on your pictures alone. You're in desperate need of some discipline, aren't you?"

I'm glad he's following me down this daddy rabbit hole because the types of discipline he might mete out sounds intriguing. "Only from you."

"Listen, I need to think about what to do with you." His hands drop to my ass before turning to shove me against the wire racks holding the cafe snacks and extra drinks. It shakes at the impact, the hard metal digging into my back. "I haven't exactly gone through the employee handbook, but there's bound to be a rule against a superior dating his subordinate. Once I find out what the protocol is, then we can discuss next steps."

"But —"

Thomas's hand lands a light slap to my left butt cheek, and I jump at the contact, pushing my core into his hard erection — not something I'm mad about. "No buts. You're going to do as I say and behave until I say it's safe. Until I know it's okay for me to strip you bare and fuck this tight cunt while you scream my name. Understand?"

Struggling for breath, I force the

two words I've been imagining aloud. "Yes, Daddy."

His eyes widen while his fingers clench my ass in a firmer grip. "You're going to be a handful, aren't you?" But he doesn't sound upset. No, there's an anticipation in his expression that makes my legs go weak. Bending down, he crushes another kiss to my mouth before reluctantly pulling away and leaving me alone — stunned and burning for more of his touch.

Once I've recovered sufficiently to connect coherent sentences, I text Ella and Abigail the bombshell news of meeting my mystery man, and we agree to meet for dinner at my place to discuss this wild development. The lights blink out in the cafe as I shut everything down for the afternoon. It's my usual routine, yet it feels odd performing such a mundane task as if my world wasn't shaken to the ground in the past hour.

I went from having a relationship

on paper and worrying about it changing if we met to meeting Thomas and calling him, "Daddy." I guess I really have run out of fucks to give because the speed my mind and body got on board with the change threatens to give me whiplash.

Fifteen minutes later, I've changed into comfier clothes and lounge on the couch when a series of knocks rap on my front door. Ella and Abigail stand on the tiny wooden platform acting as my porch with bags of Chinese in their hands.

"Thank god, you're here. I'm starving and desperate to share what happened today." They hurry inside, and we divy up the food before settling in the living room, their eager faces trained on me.

"Okay, give it up. Your new boss is your pen pal?" Ella stuffs a forkful of fried rice in her mouth, the diamond ring on her hand flashing in the lamplight. She'd found love with her longtime crush — her brother's best friend, Gavin — and was now happily engaged.

"Yep, and he's a bit of a silver fox." Their brows raise in mutual surprise before Abigail fans herself.

"Really? I take it that's not a problem for you?"

"When I set the age range on the dating apps I used to have, I kept it within a five year limit. But now that I've met Thomas, and we've learned so much about each other, the age difference doesn't really bother me. And I kind of like the taboo nature of it."

"You're welcome for sharing those books with you," Abigail crows. As a librarian, she has access to thousands of books and is always recommending spicy reads. You wouldn't think by looking at her that she'd be into some of the darker romantic themes, but some of the stuff she's mentioned has made even me blush.

"So, you're hot for the boss. But

what about the other issue? Weren't you worried about speaking in person, having it ruin the nature of your relationship?"

Swallowing my mouthful of crab rangoon, I shake my head dismissively. "Not anymore. I can't explain it, but those fears melted aways once I knew who Thomas was. The guy from the letters merged with the flesh and blood man before me to create someone I know I can trust and definitely want."

Ella sighs and relaxes more into the armchair she commandeered. "That makes me happy to hear. I'm glad something good came out of that matchmaking booth, since it was such a bust for us." She motions to Abigail and herself.

"Yeah, but obviously it was never meant to work for you. Look at what happened between you and Gavin." Abigail toys with her food as a wave of sadness rolls off her slumped shoulders.

Leaning over, I pat her knee in encouragement. "Don't worry. Your turn is next. Maybe Gavin or Thomas have a single friend. Then, you can be like me and have a sexy, older man for yourself." I wink playfully, hoping to cheer her up.

"Doubtful, but I'll try to keep hope alive. Though, it's not terrible surviving on book boyfriends alone."

"Book boyfriends can only get you so far. Trust me, you want a real man between your legs instead of a battery-operated machine." Ella points out and takes another bite from the carton of food in her hand.

"Ella!"

"Oh my god!" I giggle in amusement. "Gavin's really done a number on you with his dirty talk. I can't believe you said that."

Normally, I'm the one with the outrageous one-liners, but I appreciate how much she's come out of her shell since getting together with Gavin. And I wonder how much I'll change with Thomas, already I've become more confident, and that was before we officially met. Excited for the future, I focus on my best friends as the rest of the night devolves into laughter while we discuss what I should do about Thomas's rules for our relationship before switching to Ella's wedding plans.

But in the back of my mind, I consider what tomorrow will bring, and a naughty plan forms for how to get Thomas on board with us.

CHAPTER FOUR

THOMAS

Two days pass while I struggle with deciding what to do about Saoirse. I've avoided returning to the cafe and thrown myself into work, but my curvy little redhead is never far from my mind. Damn, is she sexy and sweet.

And off-limits until you figure out what to do.

Stifling a groan of annoyance at the predicament we find ourselves in, I enter the mailroom and check my cubby to see a stack of flyers along with an envelope with my name written in cursive on the front. I recognize those feminine swirls, and heat rises in my blood. Surely, she wouldn't risk sending one of her explicit letters here. Right? Especially after I warned her to behave.

Tossing the unwanted flyers into the recycling bin, I tuck the letter in my coat pocket and hustle back to my office for privacy. "Hold any calls, Kelsey," I say before closing the door and ripping the letter open.

The note is short: *When daddy doesn't want to play, toys make my day.*

Nose flaring in need, my eyes drop to the attached polaroid. Saoirse sits in the middle of her bed surveying the collection of sex toys laid out in a half circle. With knees tucked underneath her and the sheer pink babydoll nightgown clinging to her curves, she's clearly going full tilt with this daddy and little girl theme. But I can't deny my own lust for the dynamic as I picture tugging on those loose pigtails trailing over her shoulders while I fuck her with my cock and that pink vibrator I spy in the corner.

Desire floods my shaft, and my palm twitches to spank the little brat for tempting me while at work. The cafe's still open which means she's down there besieged with students, but rational thinking has disappeared as I stuff the picture and note back into my pocket and head that way.

Marching into the cafe, a line of customers wrap around the counter, talking and checking out the menu. Saoirse must be in the kitchen because I don't see her tending the register, so I maneuver through the crowd of teens and pass the barista on my way back. The poor kid looks confused, so I flash my school ID as if I have a reason to be here.

Another employee mans a row of blenders while Saoirse refills a canister with some powdered mix. "Ms. Shane, a word, please?" I bite out the words, trying to contain the lust and fury radiating from my bones, but it's clear she understands why I'm here — if her satisfied smile is anything to go by.

"We're a bit busy at the moment, Mr. Moore. Perhaps at a later time?" She ignores my request, continuing to pour the powder from its original bag into the large marked container.

Before I can argue, the girl pouring a smoothie from a blender pipes up. "Oh, it's alright. I've got things covered if you need to go."

"Thank you." I nod towards the girl and motion for Saoirse to precede me out the back door leading to the gravel parking lot behind the building. Seeing it empty, I explode. "You think this is smart? This is exactly why we can't be together if you're going to pull stunts like this!" I snatch the photo out of its hiding place and wave it in the air. "Anyone could've seen this. You risked yourself for what? To prove a point?"

Defiant arms cross over her chest as her chin lifts in challenge. "What, you didn't like it?"

"It doesn't matter if I liked it or not. It doesn't belong in my work mailbox when I directly told you to wait until I figure out what the school policies are for our situation." The handbook mentioned how relationships between employees are discouraged when I read it after our first meeting, but it didn't say anything else or go into consequences if someone broke the unofficial rule.

"Well, you're taking too long, and since *you* won't take care of my needs..." She stalks forward as if to steal the photo back, but I shove it in my back pocket. I may be angry over the way she sent it, but that doesn't mean I don't want it. The image of my little girl about to fuck herself while imagining me? Enough fuel to keep me jacking off for the rest of the goddamned week.

"What you *need* is a good spanking." And again, my hand quivers in anticipation of feeling her round ass beneath it, plump cheeks turning red from the impact.

"Are you offering?"

"Not today, little girl... But, soon. You just need to learn patience." While I need to relearn control because my head is spinning from what this restraint is costing me. Eight fucking months of letters and teasing — of foreplay, if I'm honest — and we have to wait because I decided to accept a new job as her boss. Fate can be a cruel bitch sometimes.

"Hmm... I'm not big on patience. I've waited long enough, as you well know. Doing what I want when I want is more my style these days." She tosses her hair over her shoulder and shoots a flirty smile my way before fluttering her fingers in goodbye and leaving me to stew alone in the parking lot.

God, that woman is infuriating.
And fucking mine.

CHAPTER FIVE

SAOIRSE

The crinkling of the plastic popsicle wrapper rings in my ears as I tear it off. Shoving the icy treat in my mouth, I contemplate what I'm about to do as I try to get my lips red and the popsicle dripping — imagining a sexy scene in Thomas's office.

Am I out of my mind for thinking I can seduce the man in his office after his warning? Maybe.

Am I committing job suicide by risking such a scandal on school property? Probably.

But it'll be worth it to act out this fantasy — to tease my man. Even if Thomas hasn't agreed to that title yet.

But he will. I saw how he reacted to the photo I sent him. He just needs another little push.

Checking myself in the compact mirror pulled from my purse, I hope this exaggerated coloring around my mouth looks sexy instead of clownish. *Only one way to find out.*

The hall is empty since it's after five and his office is on the third floor, separate from the larger departments. Like a stalker, I know he's been working late which is how this plan came to fruition. I want to catch him alone.

A single light shines underneath the closed door, and a twinge of fear that his secretary locked it on her way out seeps through me — knocking and having him let me in isn't on the agenda. But a breath of relief escapes as the door knob turns easily in my shaky hand. Stepping inside the communal lounge that branches into Thomas and another VP's offices, I quietly close the door behind me and turn the latch for privacy.

Nerves tingle from the tips of my toes to the ends of my wild red hair, and the electric feeling jolts me into action. Thomas's personal office door lies open, beckoning me forward.

"Working late?" I ask, strutting in with all the confidence in the world like I belong.

"Saoirse? What are you doing here?" He glances at the watch on his wrist, the strong muscles of his forearm flexing. "Shouldn't you be preparing for tonight's event?"

"All in good time. First, I wanted to see you." I prop a hip against his desk and tilt forward, my breasts pushing against the low cut of the bustier I changed into and threatening to spill out. Sliding the popsicle through the round 'o' of my mouth, I plump my lips and suck — the wet sound like a shot in the silent room.

Thomas's eyes drop from the obscene gesture to my cleavage before returning to where I release the treat with a pop. "What the hell do you think you're doing? What game is this?"

Maneuvering around the oak desk, I squeeze between his splayed legs and the firm edge of wood, forcing him to roll away to give me space. "No game. Unless you count me coming here to show you what you're missing by denying us a chance. Which is ironic when you think about it, considering you were the one pushing so hard for us to meet in person. Is this a case of needing to be careful what you wish for?" I continue licking the popsicle, enjoying the heat from his enraptured gaze as I wait for his response.

"That was before I became your boss. No, your boss's boss. Add that to the fact that you're too young for me, and it's a recipe for disaster. So, you should leave, heed the many warnings I've given you." His firm tone belies the yearning on his face; he can't fool me.

Tossing the last of the popsicle in the trash bin to the right, I grasp his chair and push until the wheels run into the wall behind Thomas. Smoothing eager hands over his sleeve-covered arms until they reach his shoulders, I rest heavily on him, giving him an eyeful down my top, and whisper in his ear. "I'm not going anywhere until I've had you in my mouth; the popsicle was just an appetizer. Practice if you will. Now, I want the real thing."

The smell of his cologne tickles my nose as my lips ghost over his clean-shaven cheek before settling over the grim line of his mouth. Gently tugging on his bottom lip, I encourage him to let me in. "Come on, just a taste. Don't you want this cherry tongue? So sweet and —"

Thomas opens with a growl, his hand tangling in my hair, as our tongues meet in a duel for dominance. Pressing closer, his head angles back in deference to my higher position, and my tongue delves deeper before I pull back — Thomas following the retreat.

"Don't worry; I'm not going anywhere." Drawing my hands down his chest, they land on his belt, and I sink to my knees, quickly undoing the belt buckle and his pants.

"We shouldn't be doing this," Thomas warns, though his hand on my neck doesn't stop me from lowering my head to the leaking tip of his cock after I release him from the restraints of his clothing. "You... Saoirse... Fuck..."

His hips buck in the chair, driving more of him into my mouth as I start to replicate my earlier actions with the popsicle. Thicker and hotter than the icy treat, I hum at the difference and wrap a hand around the base. Did sucking a man off within days of meeting ever feature in my thoughts of the future? No, but it's not like this is some one night stand.

This is Law… or Thomas — the man I've been writing and seducing for months with intimate photos. This is just the natural progression of such an extended period of foreplay.

My tongue rubs along the sensitive underside, and I look up through fringed lashes to see his fixated stare on me. "Like what you see?" The husky question purrs from my throat before I kiss along his length.

He snarls at the question. "You know I do." The hand at my neck moves to scratch at my scalp, pulling the hair taut. I whimper at the slight pain but don't stop. "You think you're in control? Like calling all of the shots between us? Just wait, little girl. I'll let you have your fun until we work out the professional logistics of our relationship. When that time comes, all bets are off."

A shiver of anticipation travels

down my spine, and I release him long enough to nod. "Whatever you say, Daddy. But your little girl's going to enjoy making you regret wanting to wait." Fire shines in my determined eyes as I dare him to end this, knowing he can't. He's right; I hold the power now, and I fucking love it. Just like I'll love it when he takes it back and bends me to his will.

God, I want that so bad.

My efforts to please him double as his shaft swells before thick jets of seed shoot down my throat and overflow the seal I have around the mushroom head, dripping down my chin. Mutual groans of satisfaction erupt as I try to swallow every drop until the spasming of his cock slows. Retreating, I wipe the excess off my chin and lick my fingers, watching the lust in Thomas's gaze flare again as he reaches for me.

Jumping to my feet, I scurry away, wagging an admonishing finger. "No, no, no. None of that. It wouldn't be appropriate. Isn't that what you like to say?"

"Saoirse, get your sexy little ass back here before I —"

"Sorry, I don't think it'd be a good idea. What if someone catches us?" I fake gasp and cover my mouth, eyes wide in exaggeration. "But I'm glad you're starting to come around to my way of thinking. Think of this tonight when you're going to bed alone and dreaming up rules to keep us apart."

With that parting jab, I exit like a queen leaving court or at least, that's how I feel until I'm far enough away to sag against a wall for support. *Holy fuck.* I really just did that. The nerves I held at bay earlier transform into an adrenaline high that makes me feel invincible.

Good thing, too, because tonight's going to be a long one with the cafe hosting the after party when the soccer game is over. I'll need all the energy I can get, but I don't think it'll be a problem now — not with the know-ledge of Thomas being putty in my hands.

CHAPTER SIX

THOMAS

The whir of the air conditioning drones in the room, and it's ridiculous that I need it this late in October. Kicking the covers off, I swipe a hand over the sweat gathered on my forehead, though most of the heat burns in my blood as I recall this afternoon.

Saoirse on her knees for me.

Saoirse sucking me off with innocent enthusiasm.

Fuck.

A tortured groan rumbles in my chest. I should've known something would go wrong with this whole matchmaking business. It went well for months only to blow up in my face by having her become my subordinate and almost fifteen years younger. The age difference I could deal with but coupled with our working together? What a mess.

And it doesn't help that she thwarts any attempts I make to keep our distance until things can be worked out.

Rolling to a sitting position, I brace my hands on the edge of the bed, frustration roiling in my stomach. And an irrepressible thought emerges. My phone shows it's after midnight which means the event at The Bean tonight should be ending soon. I skipped the homecoming game after our interlude — too wired to handle a crowd of screaming fans.

If I'm not going to be able to sleep, maybe I can catch up with Saoirse and talk.

Or repay her favor from earlier...

A picture she sent weeks ago flashes in my mind as I get up to leave: a shot down her body where a hand had slipped under pink panties. One of the riskier poses I received from her, I want to reenact the moment but with my own hand dipping between her slick folds. It's only fair after all of the teasing she's put me through this week.

The empty staff parking lot reminds me I shouldn't be here, but I shift the car into park and get out anyway. Tall lamps brighten patches of the sidewalk that leads to the student center, lit like a beacon on the otherwise deserted campus.

Glass doors showcase the decorated foyer, and a familiar redhead shuffling towards the exit, a large tote slung over her shoulder. Jogging the last few steps, I swing the door open for her and see confusion cloud her tired expression.

"Thomas? What are you doing here?"

My original plan flies out the window as she yawns, clearly exhausted. Gently prying the tote from her hands, I say, "I couldn't sleep, so I thought we could talk. But it can wait; let's just get you home. Where did you park?"

"At home." She covers another yawn. "I walked here, since my apartment's only a couple of blocks away."

That doesn't sit well. "You mean you walk home alone every night?"

"Not every night, and usually not this late unless it's a special event."

"That's not very safe." Anything could happen to her. Unprotected, she's ripe for some bastard to steal, and my fists clench, ready to punch the imaginary danger.

She scoffs at my concern. "Don't worry, it's a small town; nothing ever happens."

And it definitely won't happen now that I know your routine.

We continue walking along the street once the sidewalk ends, and I study the old homes and cars. It seems sedate, but better to be safe than sorry when it comes to my girl.

She's not yours. She can't be — not yet.

"For my peace of mind, please consider driving or let me know when you're going to be late. I'll come to walk you home safely."

"This coming from the man who thinks it's inappropriate for us to be together. Walking me home sounds suspiciously like something a partner would do."

"It'd be strictly for your protection; nothing more," I deny, knowing it for the lie it is. "But you know I'm right about us."

"And you know how I feel about being underneath you." The conversation veers away from work as Saoirse's tone shifts, and I understand her meaning. Frankly, I don't mind the dynamic either when it comes to the bedroom, but it's not good for a professional environment where her livelihood lies in my hands.

"You're not thinking clearly. It's late; you need sleep. Then, maybe you'll see reason," I mumble. A rectangular building sits on the street corner, and I follow Saoirse as she heads towards the last of three doors.

"I don't know... I was thinking pretty clearly earlier. Do you think I saw reason after going to my knees for you? Or maybe when your cock filled my mouth?"

Once she has the front door unlocked, I urge her inside. "Damn, Saoirse. You can't say things like that. I'm barely holding it together already. Do you think this is easy for me? For months, we've written to each other. I've shared deeply personal stories, as did you, along with those sexy as hell photos. You think I want to give you up even temporarily?"

"You sure make it look easy," she grouses, stumbling into her bedroom. The apartment is tiny and looks to be separated into four quarters: a living room, kitchen, bedroom, and bathroom.

Placing a steadying arm around her waist, I drop the tote I'm carrying to the floor and guide her towards the end of her bed. "You can't even stand straight, yet you think you can reason with me? Baby, I'm going to get you ready for bed, then we'll talk tomorrow."

"I don't need your help." She kicks off her shoes before struggling to wiggle out of her jeans. This may not be the wisest choice I've ever made — staying to help her undress — but I'm not leaving.

"I think you do." Bending to yank the tight denim down her legs, a cautious grin tips my lips. She's adorable like a sleepy kitten, fighting me and her clothing.

Sighing, she flops back, arms spread wide. "Fine. I'm too tired to argue anymore. I feel so old compared to students now."

"Trust me, you're still a baby compared to me. Now, where are your pajamas?"

"Just grab one of the long tees hanging in the closet." Her hand waves haphazardly towards the miniscule closet hiding behind the bedroom door. I tug a blue tee off a hanger before turning to see her struggling to get the shirt she has on over her head. My mouth dries at the sight of her breasts, lush and heavy, held by a serviceable beige bra — a marked change from the usual underwear she shows me but no less enticing.

"Help me." A pout pushes a plump lip out, and I force my lungs to take deep breaths as I remind myself that nothing is going to happen tonight besides my getting her into bed for sleep. *And only sleep.*

Untangling the scrap of cotton from her arms, I quickly unlatch her bra after she presents her back. Covering all the pretty revealed freckles, I toss the oversized tee over her body and carefully pull her hair out from the collar, dropping a soft kiss to her neck.

"Mmm…" Saoirse tilts her head, and I can't resist kissing the spot again before massaging the tense muscles along her shoulders. It's been a long day for her and tenderness overrides the lust rushing south.

"Come on, baby. Only one more thing." Saoirse's fading fast as I lead her to the bathroom and get her toothbrush prepped. "Here you go." She brushes in slow strokes with her eyes closed, body swaying. When she's done, it's a relief to tuck her into bed.

"Don't go." Her sweet plea rends my heart in two — not to mention my conscience. But if she wants me to stay, I can't refuse her, especially when it's in line with my own needs.

Fuck it. I'll deal with the consequences tomorrow.

Flicking my shoes off, I'm beside her in two seconds flat, and she curls her soft body around mine. "Good night, baby," I whisper, closing my eyes and enjoying this moment while it lasts.

CHAPTER SEVEN

SAOIRSE

Warmth surrounds me as I float in a hazy dream of Thomas. He's tracing the skin of my cheek and arm, then a shiver runs through me as he exposes my thigh to his touch and the cooler air of the room. How far will he go?

Every night since the relationship with my mystery man was formed, I've dreamed different scenarios, fantasies of us together. Now that I know Thomas is the man, my mind can finally fit him into the starring role.

He lifts one of my legs over his shoulder as he settles between my thighs, brushing kisses over the delicate insides, and the smallest smile forms because this is already better than past imaginings. The beginnings of a beard scrape against me, and my brows furrow in confusion. Thomas doesn't have a beard. He's always clean shaven.

What does it matter if it's true to life? It's a dream. Enjoy it.

Letting go of conscious thought, I continue to drift in the pleasure — his mouth sucking the bare lips of my pussy, tongue lapping at my clit. Thomas takes his time, eating me at a leisurely pace like I'm a delicacy he wants to savor, and I appreciate the thoroughness of him and this dream.

My hips gently arch, my heel digging into his back, desperate for more, and his name sighs out on a breathy whimper. "Thomas."

My orgasm peaks all at once, the patient building of tension released in a bright burst of potent relief that ebbs into soothing waves despite the insistent flicking of Thomas's tongue, causing my body to jerk again in response.

"Good morning, baby." The male, sleep-roughened voice doesn't sound like a figment of my imagination, and neither does the addition of his fingers probing my wet entrance. Cracking my eyes to slits, I see Thomas staring at me, a tenderness in his gaze that makes my heart melt.

This is real. Holy fuck.

"You're still here," I say stupidly, struggling to fight the brain fog from the orgasm and sleep.

"Apparently." He shakes his head before glancing down to his lazily pumping fingers, a quiet sucking sound becoming obvious. "I woke up and couldn't leave without touching you, though I didn't mean for it to escalate this far."

"I'm glad it did." Drawing a finger down his shadowed cheek, I joke. "And this was a nice surprise. I'm not used to seeing you so unkempt."

"Sorry if it was too rough."

"It's okay… Are you going to fuck me with your cock now?" The needy question pops out as I continue to ride his fingers.

"Is that what you want?"

"Yes, please." More than anything I need the connection of him inside me. To be taken by my man.

He slides his fingers out. "Open up." Once I follow the dictate, he slips them into my mouth for me to lick him clean — the naughty act of tasting myself on him making me hotter.

"I suppose it would be a shame to waste all this sweetness," he muses, and I hum in agreement. *A real shame.* Thomas quickly undresses and strokes his hardness, staring at me contemplatively, and I worry he's going to change his mind.

Stretching an arm out in supplication, I whisper, "Come to me."

His brown eyes meet mine, an unspoken conversation passing between us, before his large body crawls over mine. "Why can't I resist you?" The muttered question becomes muffled as our mouths meet in a passionate kiss.

Because you love me.

My hopeful prayer twinkles in and out like a shooting star, etching out the realization that whatever his feelings, I *do* love him. This week may be defined by sexual innuendos and physical intimacy, but there's a deeper connection woven over the better part of a year through our letters. We didn't start strictly sexual; we began with stories of our lives and dreams of the future. It's only natural that our physical connection would be so feverish — intense to match the emotional depth.

Thomas grinds his erection between my thighs, and I spread them wider, urging him to dip lower. "You're like candy. Sweet and addictive. I can't get enough." His tongue licks along my neck, hands dragging my tee off, before sucking one of my nipples into the heat of his mouth. Teeth gently hold it in place while he flicks and prods the sensitive tip, and I scratch at his back, needing him to focus on where I need him — my empty pussy.

"Thomas, stop teasing. I need you now." The desperate appeal accompanies the thrust of my hips, and the tip of his cock brushes against my opening.

"Remember what I said about patience?" He switches to my other nipple, and I grunt in annoyance.

"Fuck patience. You need to fuck me now or else —"

Thomas's head jerks up as a hand pushes down on my chest, holding me steady. "What was that?" Burning hunger ignites his expression. "Your time's up, little girl. I warned you what would happen, but you kept pushing. I see now that you need to be taught how to behave. Turn over."

He lifts to give me room to move, and I follow the order tentatively, though sparks of heat cause my pussy to clench at what's to come.

"Hold on to your pillow, and remember you earned each and every one of these." A calloused hand smoothes over my exposed ass — the calm before the storm. When it smacks one cheek with a resounding slap, I wince but arch for more as Thomas rubs the sting away. This continues for ten alternating pats, the pain blooming outward while mewling sounds of need rumble in my throat.

"Do you need another reminder of who's in charge? Or are you going to be a good girl? " Tender kisses skim over my flaming cheeks before trailing up my spine in a soothing pattern.

"Yes, Daddy... I'll be good; I promise." *Just put me out of my misery, please.*

"Mmm... I like it when you call me

that. It sounds so pretty coming from your lips. Just like these freckles decorating your skin — a pretty map leading me to your most sensitive places." He helps me roll over, the cotton blanket scratching at my sensitive skin. "You ready for your reward?"

He circles my clit with the weeping head of his cock before dragging it down to breach my opening with one thick inch. Moaning, I tighten my pussy, trying to pull him deeper. "More... Please, fuck me, Daddy."

Thomas chuckles. "I'll give you more in my own time, little girl. Did you forget what you wrote to me? This sweet little pussy hasn't had a man in years." My mouth prepares to refute him, but he drops a quick, harsh kiss on my lips. "And those toys of yours don't count. Because I can feel how tight you are; this young cunt needs to be stretched properly. I don't want to hurt my pretty, little girl."

"You won't, I promise. Please..." I

beg, tired of balancing on the edge of relief. Sweat gathers on my forehead, and my heart's beating out of my chest. This prolonged build-up is more than anything I've experienced before, and all my talk about being with an experienced man mocks me as I lay here at his mercy.

Naive Saoirse never could've imagined being brought to the brink of pleasure like this, only for him to withhold it — to shape it into something greater than a cursory orgasm. I thank my lucky stars for that innocence because it pushed me to tempt and tease until Thomas finally gave in, showing me what I've been missing.

CHAPTER EIGHT

THOMAS

My muscles shake with the force of restraint I'm using not to slam into Saoirse and give us both what we need. Lowering my head, I lick the salt from her gleaming skin, thrilling at the tremble such a simple act sets off in her body. She's beginning to reach her limit which was my goal all along — to pleasure her so well, so thoroughly — because it might be all we have.

Allowing my hips to push forward, I sink deeper into her wet heat, something I've dreamed of doing for months. Her snug sheathe chokes my dick, and possessiveness punches me in the gut. She'd shared her bad luck with men, how awkward her past interactions were in our letters. It'd been a huge factor behind her signing up for the matchmaking booth.

I know about her one night stand years ago, and all I want to do is wipe that memory away. To prove that she's mine and mine alone.

Sliding to the hilt, a cry of shock rings out, and Saoirse's entire body shudders as an orgasm rocks through her. Pride thumps in my chest, and instinct drives me to a savage pace, riding her through the peaks of pleasure. "That's it. You're so beautiful when you come; I want to see it again. You want that, baby?"

"It's too much..." Her glazed eyes plead with me. "What... are you... doing to me?"

My hands grip the supple flesh of her hips as I furiously pump my cock, punctuating each of her dragged out words. "Loving you. Giving you what you need." *Even if it's on borrowed time.*

Tweaking a pert nipple under my thumb, I take her mouth in a blazing kiss of ownership before her body locks me in a crushing embrace, and we both tumble over the edge into oblivion. Spent, my arms give out as I collapse in her arms, soft curves cradling me in contentment.

"You sure know how to show a girl a good time." Saoirse quips, panting for breath.

Nuzzling her neck where strands of damp curls cling to the skin, I mumble, "And you're sure to be the death of me, but I suppose we all have our burdens to bear."

Her hand combs through my short hair in lingering strokes that send a soothing surge of comfort through my tired limbs. It's a good thing it's Saturday or else we both would be fucked because there's no way I could force myself from this bed — from her — to go to work.

Work.

The place where I'm her boss.

The institution that discourages these types of liaisons.

Saoirse brushes gentle pecks over my face and smiles. "It wouldn't be such a terrible way to go, right? After all, you'll be with me." She continues to cuddle into me, and I decide to take this weekend for myself — for us. Come Monday, it'll be back to reality, but today and tomorrow?

I'm going to soak in as much time as possible with my girl.

Time passes like the last grains of sand in a timer: fast and unstoppable. Saturated with love and laughter, Saoirse and I spent most of the weekend in her bed after I grabbed some clothes from home, though we took a couple of brisk walks in the fall weather that finally chose to make an appearance. It felt like we were a normal couple, enjoying each other's company, despite the storm clouds on the horizon.

Before I knew it, Sunday night arrived along with the moment I needed to let Saoirse know we couldn't continue. Bracing for her reaction, I finish zipping up my jacket before leaving and say the four dreaded words. "We need to talk."

"Oh, my favorite line." She sits on the arm of her couch, one leg swinging in agitation. "Let me guess: this was a one-time deal, we shouldn't be doing this?"

"You know I'm right. Until I speak with HR, it's not a good idea."

"I swear, Thomas, you sound like a broken record. You don't even believe the crap you're spewing because if you did, you wouldn't have spent the weekend fucking me against every available surface in this apartment."

"I admit I haven't been very good at maintaining a distance, and I'm not saying this will be forever. But if we get caught messing around without notifying the proper people, we put both of our jobs in jeopardy. I just think we should be smart about this." Tomorrow I'll approach Mr. Patton, the man who hired me, and hear what the next course of action should be. Hopefully, we'll sign a document or get a verbal approval, and the matter will be settled.

"God, do you hear yourself? Jobs are expendable; we're not. You're more important to me than managing a college cafe; I'm sure I could find something else if need be. But your whole focus is following the rules instead of your heart, and I don't know if that's what I want in a partner." She runs a hand through her hair in frustration before shrugging in surrender. Ice forms in my veins at the threat of losing her.

"I'm being practical, protecting both of our interests. Why can't you see that?"

"Maybe I'm too young or naive because to me it looks like you're running scared. Letting some arbitrary policy dictate your life." Saoirse juts out her chin in defiance. "And I told you: I do what I want when I want. I've lived by the rules my entire life, and all it's done is hold me back. That part of my life is over — either get on board or get out."

"So, that's it? Your way or nothing?" I scoff and rip the door open, hiking the duffel bag of my stuff over a shoulder. "You really are a child, aren't you? Maybe try taking a nap, perhaps it'll remove those rose-colored glasses you're wearing and help you see sense when tomorrow dawns."

Stomping out, I close the door with a click, too frustrated to keep arguing. Especially when she's set on denying sound reasoning. Tomorrow I'll fix things. Get our approval and move past this hiccup in our relationship.

Until then, home awaits along with a pile of work that needs to be done, since I've neglected it all weekend. Maybe it'll help cool my blood by doing something productive.

Not fucking likely.

CHAPTER NINE

SAOIRSE

Nausea roils around in my stomach. After the past forty-eight hours, Thomas still plans on keeping me at arms length. How can he so easily dismiss the intimate bond that strengthened between us beyond the letters?

Tears of disappointment well up as I lock the door after his departure and retire to my room. The messy bed is an unwanted reminder of our extended goodbye — making love blissfully unaware that everything would blow up in such quick succession.

Texting Ella and Abigail, I relay the latest drama and wonder if this isn't what we were meant to be all along. Instead of believing Thomas was the one for me, maybe he's really just a stepping stone — his only purpose to help me grow in confidence, to trust myself around men. The thought tightens my stomach in despair.

"Don't give up hope yet," Abigail encourages, including a hug and heart emoji in her message.

"Remember the trouble I had with Gavin? We made it through, and so will you. Just give him time." Ella's pointed reminder about Gavin makes me feel a little better. Like Thomas, he held reservations about pursuing Ella since she's his best friend's little sister, but they worked it out in the end.

The irony of my situation strikes me as I consider how I've been coaxing Thomas into this relationship — how the tables have reversed. A letter never went by without a plea to meet being mentioned by him, and now I can't get him to commit. His worries about the college aren't unfounded, but I wish he'd choose me first. Then, we can approach HR together as a team, show that this isn't some fling they can dismiss.

Perhaps you should have told him that instead of flying off the handle.

Rubbing a hand over my wet cheek, I let loose an inelegant snort. Yeah, that might've been the better plan. But my temper got the best of me, and I started saying things I didn't really mean — building myself into a fervor when I should've stayed calm and discussed things like an adult.

Tomorrow's a new day, I reason. I'll apologize to Thomas and agree to do what he thinks is best even if it does rankle. Relationships are about compromise, right?

After dropping off my purse and work tote in The Bean, I skip up the stairs of the student center to head towards Thomas's office. It's a dreary day, a bit of a let down after the hype of last week, but the chilly weather suits my mood. Stuffing cold hands in my pockets, I cross the quad when I recognize the man shuffling towards me.

"Thomas? I was just coming to see you."

"Great minds think alike because I was doing the same. Come with me." He grabs a hand from my pocket and twines his fingers with mine before hauling me behind him back to the main office building.

"Whoa, slow down. I want to apologize for yesterday. I didn't mean for things to get so heated, and nonsense kind of blurted out." The words huff out in a rush as his pace never falters; my short legs scrambling to take two steps for every one of his.

"I'm sorry, too. Last night, my

mind was racing for a solution, re-playing our conversation. And I realize I've been a bit harsh." He stops long enough to cup my cheek and press a rough kiss to my lips. "You were right. I've barely begun this job; it's not like I'm entrenched in this community. I'll call up one of the other offers I received and see if they're still available if we can't be together here."

Joy encompasses my soul at the words I've longed to hear. "You'd do that for me? Quit your job?" It's not something I want for him, but I appreciate the fact that he's willing to make such a drastic change.

"Baby, I'd do anything for you. I just haven't done a good enough job of showing you lately, but that stops today." Thomas drags the building door open, and we hustle down the hall past a string of offices.

"Where are we going? I want to kiss you and tell you how much I love you and —" My free hand covers a gasp of surprise at the declaration. I didn't mean to spring it on him like this — in the middle of a musty hall.

But it has the desired effect because Thomas jerks to a halt and faces me, a wild look in his eyes. "What did you say?"

Curious stares skitter over us as two members of staff walk by, and embarrassment burns my cheeks. Avoiding his gaze, I glance down at my feet, the toe of my converse tapping against the worn carpet. "I'm sorry if it's too fast, and this really isn't very romantic. Surrounded by colleagues."

"Tell me what you said, Saoirse. Now," he demands. "I need to hear those words from you again."

A trembling hand cups my cheek, forcing my face upward to clash with the determined expression on his. "I love you, okay?"

"Okay." He grins, tracing my eyebrow with his thumb. "Because I love you, too. Now, let's get this over with, so I can show you how much."

"But what are we doing?" The question gets lost as we start moving, but my feet barely feel like they're touching the ground. Thomas loves me. After a whirlwind week of push and pull, he admitted it, and I'm not letting him take it back — no matter what happens.

"Doing what I should've done that first afternoon I knew my Liberty was really the adorable cafe manager, Saoirse."

My nose wrinkles in confusion before understanding dawns as we enter Mr. Patton's office. A medium bronze plaque on the wall reads "Human Resources", and my blood pumps faster from recognition.

Guess I should've been more careful what I wish for because here we are — together — about to confront our future like the team I wanted to be.

Somehow, I forgot to factor in how fucking scary this would be.

Thomas interprets my sudden hesitation correctly and squeezes my hand in comfort. "Don't worry. Everything will be okay, trust me. You're mine despite what we learn today."

His reassurance buoys me, and I nod — prepared to face whatever comes next.

CHAPTER TEN

THOMAS

"Can I help you?" Mr. Patton's assistant peers over his computer monitor upon our entrance.

"We need to speak with Mr. Patton if he's available." A swirling tornado of emotions batters my insides while we wait for the assistant to reply. Saoirse confessed her love for me. My brain struggles to comprehend that the woman of my dreams is mine.

"He'll see you now; go on in." Sweeping through the doorway, we come to an abrupt halt, and Mr. Patton's eyes drop to our clasped hands before gesturing to two chairs in front of his desk.

"Take a seat. You have an important matter to discuss, I presume?"

"Yes." We stick to standing as I explain. "Ms. Shane and I have a personal relationship you need to be aware of. It extends beyond my arrival to Smithfield and the acceptance of my position. As far-fetched as it sounds, we participated in the matchmaking booth last Valentine's Day and matched, though our true identities remained a secret until last week."

I pause for a breath and attempt to gauge the man's response to the revelation, but his stoic expression remains — eyes bouncing between Saoirse and I. "I'll resign if needed, since the employee handbook mentions how this sort of thing is discouraged."

"No need for that." Mr. Patton shakes his head and swings around to a file cabinet behind his desk. "While the theatrics of storming in here to declare your intentions was entertaining, the two of you just need to fill out a form releasing the school from any liability for issues that arise if the relationship ends."

It's a bit anticlimactic after building this moment into a make or break deal for us all week, but simple paperwork over a stern reprisal is preferred any day. Berating myself for prolonging our distress instead of taking care of the matter last week, I chalk it up to the effects of being sideswiped by the appearance of Saoirse in my life. The woman scrambles my thoughts and emotions. Is it any wonder I wasn't able to think clearly?

Mr. Patton lays identical sheets of paper on his desk and offers us pens. "Sign here, and you're all set. Though, we do prefer you keep any public displays of affection to a minimum, since this is still an academic environment."

"Of course," Saoirse murmurs, a

note of mischief in her voice. No doubt she's taken the rule as a challenge to break and see how many times we can get away with it. Amusement and anticipation fuse together as I fantasize about all the fun we're going to have: her misbehaving and me intent on disciplining her. Ducking my head to hide the expectant smile, I sign my name quickly before we leave with HR's blessing.

"Told you there was nothing to worry about," she teases once we're alone in my office a few minutes later.

"You were right; I was wrong. I accept my error in judgment." My hands lift in surrender before I wrap my arms around her waist.

"Good because you should probably learn that ninety-nine percent of the time I'm right." Her hands wind around my neck, kneading the muscle, as she grazes her breasts over my chest. *Already trying to break the rules...*

"That's a high percentage. Someone's a little cocky now that you've gotten your way." I nip at her tender earlobe and lick along the exposed line of her neck. The familiar scent of lemon tickles my nose again, and the tartness matches my girl. Like one of those sour candies, she's naughty then nice, but I'll withhold that comparison from her earshot.

"Hmm... What are you going to do to knock me down a peg?"

"Show you who's boss."

Shiny curls bounce as she throws her head back in a laugh of delight. "Do your worst. But make it quick, I don't want to get in trouble with the man in charge for missing work." She winks, knowing full well I'd never seriously reprimand her.

Swinging her around, we land on the small loveseat along one wall. "I'll make an exception."

Our mouths meet in a boisterous mashing of tongues and teeth, heavy breathing filling the room. My assistant, Kelsey, could walk in, but I don't care. I've finally got my mystery woman in my hands, and I'm never letting go.

EPILOGUE ONE

THOMAS

FOUR MONTHS LATER

Valentine's Day is back, but this time I don't need matchmaking services. Though, Saoirse and I decide to revisit the booth that started it all, as a sort of thank you to the love gods.

We're joined by her friends who I've gotten to know over the past few months. Ella is friendly and down to earth, while I bonded with her boyfriend over a mutual obsession over football. The quietest of the bunch, Abigail, is still shy around me despite Saoirse's encouragement, but her hesitance doesn't bother me. She needs time to feel comfortable, and that's okay. It reminds me of the earlier letters between Saoirse and I. That first batch of correspondence was stilted and awkward before she learned to trust and share as I persisted in writing to her.

"Can you believe it's been a year already? So much has happened since we were last here." Saoirse runs a finger down a plastic frame holding pictures of happy couples — success stories from past years. Our own photo is somewhere in the bunch after we officially told the coordinators we were ready to end the anonymity aspect of our letters. To say they were relieved to be cut out as middle man is an understatement. Apparently, we set the record for longest-running relationship to maintain its privacy. Most couples opted to learn the true identity of their match only a few weeks in.

"Time flies when you're in love?"

She slaps my arm playfully at the joke. "You can be so cheesy at times, but I'll concede that you might have a point." Studying the images of couples, she asks, "You know, you never told me why you chose the pseudonyms you did. Why did you pick Law?"

"I thought that would be obvious with my code of discipline."

She blushes at the reminder of our lovemaking last night where she'd received a spanking for misbehavior — sending another naughty picture through our work mail. "Ah, that makes sense. Liberty and Law."

"These matchmakers might have been on to something pairing us together."

"Opposites attract?"

"Definitely," I say, hugging her in a strong embrace.

Saoirse belongs to me. She's my sexy pin-up. My little girl. The fiery redhead who holds my heart in the palm of her hand. And I wouldn't have it any other way.

EPILOGUE TWO

SAOIRSE

ONE YEAR LATER

"Don't stop, Daddy! Fuck me harder, please..." My hands clutch the headboard for stability as Thomas pounds into me from behind. It's our two-year anniversary of being matched, and the morning after he proposed in an elaborate scheme with the help of Ella and Abigail.

"You beg so prettily, little girl.

Makes me want to see how good you can be if I slow down." His movements match his words, and I groan at the decreased pace, the drag of his hard cock against my walls agony. "Make you wait until you're hoarse from crying for your daddy to ride this cunt so hard you won't be able to walk today. But don't worry, I'll lick it better. You want that, pretty girl? Want my tongue lapping at this needy clit."

Thomas's thumb swipes over the swollen nub, and I shudder on the precipice. I love and loathe when he does this — takes me to the edge before pulling back, working my frayed nerves into a frenzy over and over again.

"Yes, I want it all. Need you."

He sucks at the side of my neck, hard enough to leave a bruise, and my sweaty palms cling tighter to the wooden slats of the headboard. "You have it. All that I am. You're never going to want for anything, baby. Understand?"

Love bursts in my chest at the declaration. When he delivers these promises, I always become a mountain of hormones, and gratitude that's he's mine swallows me whole. "Yes, Daddy."

Grunting in acceptance, he accelerates his pace again and doesn't stop until I do exactly as he says: cry for him as the swell of my climax snaps the tension in my body. Thomas quakes at my back, his own orgasm rolling through him in a gush of hot seed that slides down my thighs.

Crumpling to the bed, our strained inhalations are the only sound until I manage to smooth a kiss over his rapidly beating heart before hauling myself out of bed.

"Where are you headed?" Thomas snags me by the arm, and I fall back into him with an exhausted laugh.

"Today's the photoshoot with Ella and Abigail, remember?" In honor of the ten-year anniversary for the Tees &

Jeans club, we decided to commemorate the occasion with a fun photoshoot in our tell-tale uniform. Something I need to shower and change into if I don't want to be late.

"I forgot that it was today in all of the excitement. Now, I'm considering what your photoshoots usually entail," he growls, nipping my ear. "I don't have anything to worry about, do I?"

"Hmm… Don't worry. It's fully-clothed, but wait until you see what's underneath."

"That sounds promising. Want to give me a preview?" His hand skims over my stomach to cup my breast, pinching the engorged tip. Allowing him to play with me a moment more, I moan, shaking my head.

"And ruin the surprise?" I escape his grasp with a lighthearted slap to the arm. Though we've been together for a year, two if I count our first letter exchange, I still sneak illicit photos into his view. It's a fun game that keeps our relationship exciting while providing me the outlet I need. I love taking the photos as much as Thomas enjoys receiving them. They make me feel sexy and feminine along with a boost of pride that comes with making my man all hot and bothered.

Letting me go, Thomas falls back on the bed, flinging an arm over his head. "Fine, go meet your friends. I'll just be here thinking up all the ways I'm going to love you when you get back."

"Sounds like a good use of your time." I grin, excitement burgeoning in my stomach. We can't seem to get enough of each other despite the after-effects of our lovemaking still glowing on my skin.

Jumping in the shower, I send up a prayer of thanks for the gift of Thomas — the love of my life. And all because I took a risk at a silly festival.

A matchmaker's booth on Valentine's Day. Who'd have thought?

THANKS FOR READING!

Please consider leaving a rating/review on Amazon and/or Goodreads. Ratings & reviews are the #1 way to support an indie author like me.

They don't have to be long or even positive (though I hope you enjoyed this book!). All the Amazon/Goodreads algorithms care about are QUANTITY.

The more reviews, the more Amazon/Goodreads show my books to other potential readers!

And they serve as guides to readers on whether or not to take a chance on an indie author.

So, I appreciate your support!

XO, Hallie

CURIOUS ABOUT ELLA'S STORY?

Check out the first book in the Tees & Jeans series!

The Brother Bias

From the moment Ella Johnson met Gavin Cross, she knew it was love. Older, sexy, and a popular jock, everything about him gets her hot and bothered. There's only one problem...

Gavin's her brother's best friend and doesn't notice her — the curvy nerd crushing on him.

But now Ella's all grown up and unexpectedly stuck living with him for the next week. Can she gather enough courage to finally make a move or will fear stop her from getting the man she's always wanted?

Warning: This brother's best friend doesn't know what hits him when the shy girl he knew transforms into a curvy bombshell with a few naughty secrets. Get ready for steamy nights where the line between desire and loyalty blur in a story of second chances!

BOOKS BY THIS AUTHOR

Batter Up

Darcy Evans is trying to live a full, happy life. Would she move across the country with no plan if she wasn't? Yet doubt over her attractiveness stops her from taking risks when it comes to men. Until a determined baseball team owner makes his interest known and brings into question all she's believed true about herself.

Corbin Montgomery works hard to ensure his baseball team's success, and that includes attending every home game where he sees the curvy girl of his dreams. On a hot summer evening at the stadium, can he convince the shy Darcy to give him a chance?

Warning: Get ready for a grand slam of heat with instalove galore between this curvy girl and the man who wants her for himself. Oh, and did I mention we've got two virgins itching to cash in those V-cards with the right person? Step up to the plate for some hot summer lovin'!

Wood Lessons

Anna needs a change. Her routine's become a cycle of work and home -- a true hermit's lifestyle. But with a new move and job, she's ready to build the dream life she's always wanted which starts with having a home perfect for hosting friends. The first step? Commission a custom piece of furniture that leads to a fated meeting with the handsome carpenter.

Peter enjoys working with his hands. Woodworking has always been a calm escape for him until loneliness threatens his peace. But how's he supposed to find a woman holed up in his shop? Perhaps fate will have her find him because the curvy Anna looks to be just what he needs to warm up his empty bed.

When Peter offers to teach Anna "wood lessons", the match is struck for a steamy union!

Warning: A hot man in plaid meets the curvy girl of his dreams for an instalove so sweet, it's sure to make your teeth ache. Watch these two lonely people discover a love and passion that'll leave you sweating!

ABOUT THE AUTHOR

Hallie Bennett

 Hallie prefers steamy, insta-love stories where the curvy, shy, overlooked girl gets the guy. And when she ran out of reading material, she decided to write her own stories. If you want a quick, hot read, she's your girl!

Follow on Instagram: @authorhallieben-nett

Printed in Great Britain
by Amazon

18224313R00068